Journey
to the
Name Maker

Maxine Johone-Smith

Illustrated by Joanna Scott

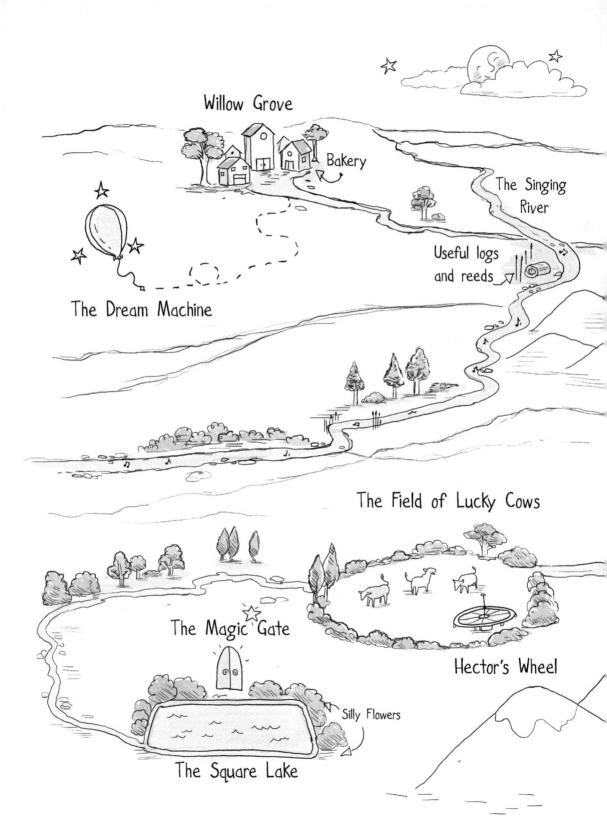

Matador
Unit E2 Airfield Business Park,
Harrison Road, Market Harborough,
Leicestershire. LE16 7UL
Tel: 0116 2792299
Email: books@troubador.co.uk
Web: www.troubador.co.uk/matador
Twitter: @matadorbooks

ISBN 978 1805140 245

British Library Cataloguing in Publication Data.
A catalogue record for this book is available from the British Library.

Printed and bound by CPI Group (UK) Ltd, Croydon, CR0 4YY
Typeset in 14pt Times New Roman by Troubador Publishing Ltd, Leicester, UK

Matador is an imprint of Troubador Publishing Ltd

FSC
www.fsc.org
MIX
Paper | Supporting
responsible forestry
FSC® C013604

With the wind whispering in his ears, he followed
its direction and crossed the cobbled square,
turned left down the sideways lane, right onto
the bendy road and into the fields beyond.
"Feathers carry dreams," the professor had said.

Contents

Chapter 1 –
Willow Grove

It was a stormy night in Willow Grove. The rain lashed at the rooftops and the wind howled in discontent. High above the clouds, the moon shivered as he sat cold and lonely, in the dark night sky. Across the cobbled square, a light flickered in the window of the old bakery. Within, all was still. The embers of the fire danced on the chimney breast like tiny stars blinking in the darkness as the fire fought against the night and struggled to stay awake. The shadows of the day stretched and yawned as they too prepared to sleep. Next to the fire, basking in its warmth, was an old coal bucket – but this was no ordinary coal bucket – this one was painted in the colours of the rainbow and had little baskets of yellow and white flowers hanging off the edge. Inside the bucket, tucked away under the shadow of the rim, barely visible from the outside world, was a tiny straw mattress covered with a little patchwork quilt which was made from old marmalade jar labels stitched together with string.

On top of the quilt, snuggled up in a woolly old sock, was the scruffiest little bear you've ever seen; his fur was sticking out in all directions, his bow was half undone around his neck, and his pyjamas were on inside out and back to front. On one side of the little mattress, there was a stack of marmalade jars, some of which were half full, and some of which were half empty. On the other side of the mattress was a small table with a crumpled old picture on top. The picture was of a snow-covered Christmas tree, draped in multi-coloured fairy lights, with a big pile of presents wrapped in shiny gold paper sitting underneath. It was time for bed. Every night before he went to sleep, the scruffy little bear would gaze at his picture and fill his head full of Christmas thoughts so he could dream of Christmas trees and presents and chestnuts roasting on the open fire while it snowed steadily outside.

Scamp had never seen a real Christmas tree, or snow, and he had never had a present wrapped in shiny gold paper, so all he could do was dream about it in the hope that one day his dreams might come true. Closing his eyes, the little bear sighed as he wriggled deeper into his sock ready to sleep, but tonight sleep wouldn't come, there were too many other thoughts racing around inside his head and no matter what he did he just *couldn't* make them go away. Tossing from side to side, he scratched his unruly fur as his eyes twinkled with curiosity in the stillness of the night. *Why am I called Scamp?* he thought. *I don't look like a Scamp, I don't feel like a Scamp, so then why am I called Scamp?* It was a question he had asked himself many times before, but tonight as the moon rode high in the sky, he was determined to find the answer.

In the opposite corner of the bakery, the Professor was preparing to sleep and as he did so, so did time. The Professor was a very old, very wise grandfather clock. No one knew for sure how old he was, but Scamp guessed that he must be at least one hundred years old because he was sooooo clever and sooooo wise, and he seemed to know everything about everything. Just that morning, there was a terrible commotion in the town, when all of the clocks had mysteriously stopped working. Everyone was confused, and didn't know what time of day it was, so they had come to see the Professor to ask for his advice.

The Professor had waved his hands and simply replied, "My dear people, there is no right or wrong time, time is an invention by which we choose to live our lives, but really it is up to us to decide what time it is. If we are hungry, then it's time to eat, if we are tired, then it's time to sleep, and if we are sad, it's time to have some fun!"

"So!" he had said, clapping his hands together. "Is anybody hungry?"

"Oh yes," replied the townspeople.

"In that case, I say it must be time for something to eat. What do you all say?"

The town's people had agreed, and without further discussion, they had followed the Professor to the old bakery, where they had all sat down to enjoy a hearty serving of afternoon tea and cakes.

The Professor knows best, thought Scamp. It was time for some action, it was time that he found the answers to his questions. Wriggling out of his sock, he peeped over the edge of his coal bucket and sniffed at the night air. It was getting dark inside the old bakery; the fire was barely awake and he could hear the sleepy sounds of the night. Trying to be as quiet as possible, he tiptoed across to the other side of the room, until he was standing directly in front of the Professor, who was busy adjusting his chimes for the morning whilst reciting his three o'clock times table.

"Three plus five is five past three, three plus ten is ten past three, three plus fifteen is quarter past three…"

"Excuse me, Sir," said Scamp, as he tapped on the Professor's door, "I'm sorry to bother you, I know it's late but I just can't sleep. I've got so many questions running around inside my head and they're making an awful lot of noise. I was hoping that you might be able to help me find the answers. They've been in my head for a very long time and they just *won't* go away."

The Professor looked down at the little bear and smiled. *What a scruffy little bear he was!*

"Well, my friend, I would be glad to help, but first, could you tell me what is troubling you at this late hour?"

Scamp took a deep breath and scratched at his nose with his paw.

"Well, Professor, it's like this you see, I would like to know why I am called Scamp. I don't think that I look like a Scamp whereas you, you look like a professor and all my friends, well, they all look like who *they* are."

Standing on tiptoe so no one else could hear, he whispered in his ear, "I think that I may have been given the wrong name."

"I see," said the Professor, fiddling with his chimes. "This *is* serious."

Bending his head so he could look the bear in the eye, the Professor continued, "Far away in the distance, over the fields and hills, is a place full of hopes and dreams; a place as beautiful as you can imagine. It is the place where dreams are made and answers are found. It is called the Dream Machine."

"The Dream Machine," repeated Scamp, his eyes widening as he spoke. "I have heard of it, but I have also heard that no one can ever find it because they always fall asleep before they get there!"

"This is true," said the Professor, scratching his face at eleven o'clock. "It is not easy to find, I know, but if you really want to know the answers to your questions, then you will need to find a way. You must leave after midnight, when all the world is asleep and dreams are being made. Feathers carry dreams, so take with you a single feather and follow its direction as it rides on the wind, and leads you to the place you need to go."

"But what does it look like and how will I know when I am there?" asked Scamp.

"It is a machine full of everything people dream about," replied the Professor. "Everyone's dreams are different but you will know when you are there. When you find it, simply empty your questions into the machine, return to your bed and go to sleep, and your dreams will give you the answers that you seek. This is all the advice I can give; the rest is up to you. Now, it is time for you to go and time for me to sleep, so goodnight my friend and good luck."

With that, the Professor relaxed his hands into the midnight position, tucked away his chimes, and closed his eyes.

Chapter 2 –

The Dream Machine

Scamp knew it was time to go. All he had to do was to empty his thoughts into the machine like the Professor had said. He knew that the closer he got to the Dream Machine, the sleepier he would feel, so he had to think of a way to stay awake. *What can I do?* he thought as he scratched his head. *I know! I can take some marmalade to eat on the way. If I'm eating, then I'm bound to stay awake. I'm always awake when I eat marmalade!* Crossing back to his coal bucket, he climbed inside, took a jar from next to his mattress and plucked a feather from his pillow. Pulling his scarf tightly around his neck, he opened the bakery door and stepped out into the night.

With the wind whispering in his ears, he followed its direction and crossed the cobbled square, turned left down the sideways lane, right onto the bendy road and into the fields beyond. "Feathers carry dreams," the Professor had said, so Scamp released his feather into the night and followed its direction as it danced in the air.

On and on he walked, following the feather and getting closer and closer to the Dream Machine. He knew he was getting close, because he was starting to feel really sleepy, so he decided to eat some marmalade to try and stay awake. But the more marmalade he ate, the more tired he felt until he was so tired, he could barely keep his eyes open.

What shall I do now? he thought, as he struggled to stay awake. *I can't fall asleep. If I did, I wouldn't reach the Dream Machine, and my answers would never be found.* He decided to ask the wind.

"What shall I do, wind?" he asked, looking up to the sky in the hope that the wind could help.

"What are you thinking?" whistled the wind in reply.

"Thinking?" said Scamp. "Well, I'm thinking about chestnuts, roasting on the open fire with snow on the rooftops and presents under the Christmas tree."

"SNOW!" bellowed the wind. "That's not going to help you now, think again!"

Standing in the cold night air, Scamp scratched his head and thought about what to do next. *What about strawberries – no that won't do it. How about Easter eggs, or marmalade? No, that won't do either. How about ice cream? No, I don't suppose that will help.* Scamp thought and thought about what he should do.

"I know! How about I walk backwards for a while and see if that helps?"

"Good idea," said the wind.

Walking backwards, with the wind blowing in his ears, Scamp could see where he had been instead of where he was going. It was so strange – he could see the past instead of the future – everything was in reverse. By walking backwards, he could see where he had gone wrong; eating the marmalade was making him sleepy, not keeping him awake, and suddenly the answer came!

I know! Scamp thought to himself. *I'll stick some marmalade onto my eyelids to keep them open. If I can't close my eyes, then I can't go to sleep. I'm always awake when my eyes are open!*

Taking the jar out of his pocket, he dipped his paw into the marmalade once again and slapped a generous portion onto each eyelid until they were well and truly stuck, then turned around to carry on his way.

With his eyes wide open, he continued to follow the feather, happy that he would stay awake. As he walked along, the smell of the marmalade was getting more and more tempting. It smelt soooo good and was making him feel very hungry.

Just a little taste, he thought, as he tried to lick marmalade from his eyelids, but his tongue wouldn't quite reach. On and on he walked, following the feather and trying to lick his eyelids as he went. He was so busy trying to lick the marmalade from his eyelids that he forgot how tired he was, and before he knew it, he could see the silver glow of something wonderful in the distance.

It looked like a giant balloon floating in the sky – a beautiful silver and pink balloon – covered in chocolates, strawberries and diamonds, which twinkled in the moonlight. Inside the balloon, Scamp could see all sorts of things floating around: there were bicycles and footballs, doll's houses and Christmas trees, racing cars and handbags.

Those must be dreams, thought Scamp!

He had done it. He had reached the place where dreams were made and answers were found! Dangling in the air on a thin silver thread was a large crystal. Floating above it, just visible in the night sky, was a large bucket surrounded by floating question marks and a big arrow made of flashing fairy lights saying "empty your thoughts in here".

Scamp was suddenly frightened. What would happen if he lost all his questions and they were never returned to him? Not only would he never get to find the answers to his questions, he wouldn't even remember the questions he wanted the answers to. The wind whispered in his ears and the feather tickled at his nose and Scamp knew what he had to do.

Gently, he began to pull on the crystal with his sticky paws, and as he did so, the Dream Bucket slowly lowered from the sky. Lower and lower it sank until there it was right in front of him. With his eyelids firmly stuck open, he held his nose, took a deep breath, then plunged his head deep inside the bucket and shook it vigorously from side to side until all his thoughts and dreams fell out.

Lifting his head from the bucket, he tried to think of something but nothing came. Satisfied that all his thoughts were well and truly emptied, he let go of the crystal and watched as the bucket was sucked up towards the sky and disappeared into the Dream Machine, taking all his unanswered questions with it.

Inside the machine, the dreams were slowly changing. Scamp could see chestnuts roasting on the fire, snow on the rooftops, and lots of presents wrapped in shiny gold paper sitting under the Christmas tree.

Those are my dreams, thought Scamp, scratching his head. *How did they get in there?*

Not really remembering the way he had come, he let the wind guide him back across the fields, up the sideways lane, down the bendy road and across the cobbled square, until he was finally safe and sound back in his coal bucket, beside the fire at the old bakery. Scamp was very confused. He knew that he had been out but he didn't remember where. He had marmalade on his eyelids and he was very tired.

As if in silent reflection of his mood, the wind subsided, the rain suddenly stopped, and a strange peace hung over Willow Grove.

Tomorrow, thought Scamp, *I will go and talk to the Professor. He will know what I should do to find my rightful name.* With that thought in mind, Scamp snuggled into his sock, tucked his head between his paws and promptly drifted off to sleep.

Chapter 3 –

Time to Go

It was Sunday morning, the sun stretched her flames, wiggled her nose and opened her eyes. All was dark outside and she couldn't see a thing.

"Oh, my lord, I've overslept!"

With a spring in her step, she bounced off her cloud and blew vigorously on her flames, over and over again until they were shining, warm and bright. As she did so, the sky got lighter and lighter until suddenly a new day was born. Huffing and puffing with all the exertion, but satisfied that the world was now awake, she sat back on her fluffy cloud and smiled for the world to see.

The light of the morning sun streamed through the bakery window. Nestled warm and snug in his coal bucket, Scamp was having the strangest dream, and lots and lots of answers were bouncing around inside his head.

'You must go on a journey to find what is yours.' 'Beware of the singing river, the smell of the music is dangerous.' 'Do not be beaten, there is always a way, just look at things from a different direction.' 'If you think it will be easy, it will lead you nowhere.' 'Cross the river and you will find your name, only when you have found it can you claim it.' 'Do you feel lucky? The answer is yes. The cows are lucky and they know best.' 'Answer no questions and tell no lies. If you can't see anything, just close your eyes.' 'Go round in circles high in

the sky, you must go deep into the Alphabet Forest to find out why.'
'Take care on your travels, if you need to rest, R is the best'…

As the sun shone brightly through the window, Scamp scratched his nose and ruffled his fur, trying to remember all that the dream had told him.

"Good morning!" bellowed the Professor, clapping his hands together. "Time to get up. Up, up, up, up, up!" he shouted.

Scamp was so warm and cosy, basking in the morning sun, that he snuggled deeper into his sock which to him was the most comfortable place in the whole world.

"Up up up up up," repeated the Professor. "Don't you know what time it is?"

"No," replied Scamp, rubbing his sticky eyes, still half asleep.

"Well, it's time to get up and time for you to go, so you'd better get a move on before you waste the day."

"Go? Go where?" replied Scamp, still half asleep.

"Why, to find your rightful name, of course," replied the Professor, scratching his face at nine o'clock.

Oh my! thought Scamp. *This is it; the time has finally come. I'd better start packing because I may be away for a very long time.*

With that in mind, he pulled out his best suitcase and filled it with everything he thought he would need.

First, I'll need some marmalade because I might get hungry, secondly, I'll need an umbrella to keep me dry in case it rains, thirdly, I'll need a blanket to keep me warm in case it snows, fourthly, I'll need a picture of myself to remind me of who I am in case I forget, and finally, I'll need some string because... well because you always need string, and besides, I like string.

With his suitcase well and truly packed tight with everything he needed, Scamp squeezed it together and fastened the buckle. Crossing to the other side of the bakery, he stood on tiptoe and gave the Professor a goodbye hug.

"Good luck, my friend," said the Professor. "Just remember to follow your dreams, they will lead you to the place you need to go."

With the Professor's words ringing in his ears, he turned to leave. He was excited about finding his real name, but at the same time he was very sad to be leaving all that he knew and loved. He would miss the Professor and his words of wisdom, he would miss his friends in the town and the games they played, and he would miss his coal bucket by the fire.

Turning towards the door with a tear in his eye, he waved goodbye to the Professor. All the town's people came out to see him off because they too knew it was time for him to go.

"I'll miss you all," said Scamp. "I'll be back." He waved as he set off on his journey.

"Goodbye old friend," shouted the townspeople. "We'll see you soon."

So off he went, shuffling down the lane as fast as his paws would carry him.

Chapter 4 –

The Singing River

Scamp walked for miles and miles. He'd never walked so far before, his little paws were getting sore with all the walking, but still he kept on. Through fields and over hills, he didn't stop for a minute, on and on he went, until he could walk no further.

"My word," exclaimed Scamp. "That's the furthest I've ever walked in my entire life. I must be somewhere by now?"

He certainly was, he had walked all the way to the Singing River. Sticking his little nose in the air, Scamp took a few deep sniffs.

Ummm, that smells good, he thought, as he walked closer to the river, sniffing with every step that he took. Riding on the wind was the sweetest melody that Scamp had ever smelt, the faintest of melodies, it smelt like apple pie and custard, and marshmallows toasting on the fire.

Closer and closer he walked. *Mmmm wonderful,* he thought.

28

"La, la, la, la, la," he hummed as the melody got stronger.

The closer he got to the river, the heavier his eyes became and the stronger the music smelt. Swaying from side to side, he began to drift deeper and deeper into the melody, until he too was being carried by the wind, closer and closer towards the river.

Suddenly, as his paws touched the water, he remembered his dream. 'Beware of the Singing River', the dream had warned. 'You must not try to cross her, or get too close, or she will take you to the riverbed from which you will never return'.

Shaking himself from the musical web, Scamp was instantly alert.

That was close, he thought, as he quickly scurried away from the river's edge.

What am I to do? If I cannot cross the Singing River then I have no choice but to turn back and go home, but I have come so far, I cannot go back now.

Dejected, Scamp sat hunched and lonely on the riverbank. Even with his paws held tightly over his nose, he could still smell the music all around him. The shadows of the day danced in the distance, taunting him to give up and return to Willow Grove, and all that was safe.

I cannot give up now, thought Scamp. *I must find a way to cross the river.*

He paced up and down, backwards and forwards. Sideways and backwards, trying to find the answer to his problem, but nothing came.

"What shall I do?" asked Scamp, looking up to the sky in the hope that the wind could help him.

"What are you thinking?" replied the wind.

"What am I thinking? Well… I'm thinking about snow again," said Scamp, feeling a little guilty because he was always thinking about snow, and Christmas, and presents under the tree.

"SNOW?" bellowed the wind. "That won't help you now. Think again!"

Oh my, thought Scamp, as he closed his eyes really tightly, and tried to think of something else.

After a few minutes, an idea came.

"I've got it! I'll stand on my head and see if that helps!" said Scamp.

"Good idea," said the wind.

So, stand on his head he did. Suddenly, the world looked different, sort of upside down and back to front. Everything seemed to be the opposite way to what it was.

Why that's it, thought Scamp. *I'll build a submarine and go under the river instead of over it, that way I can't be lured to the riverbed, because I won't smell the music!*

Jumping onto his paws, happy once again, Scamp began searching for things to make his submarine. First, he put a generous portion of marmalade up his nose so he wouldn't be able to smell the music.

Then, running to the river's edge, he plucked a reed out of the water.

I can breathe through that, he thought. *Now what shall I sail in?*

He decided to look in his suitcase, as he had packed lots of useful things in there. Rummaging through his things, he found his umbrella.

I know! I can sit on the umbrella under the water and breathe through the reed. Just one more thing, I will need something to tie to the umbrella to float on the water so I don't sink to the riverbed, so he hurried off to find some logs.

Rummaging again in his suitcase, he found the string and tied the logs to the umbrella handle.

Perfect! He had built himself a floating submarine, how strange! He opened the umbrella, then gingerly pushed it under the water, until it was just far enough under for him to sit in, then he grabbed the reed with his right paw, and sat in the umbrella under the water with the logs floating on the surface. Breathing in and out through the reed, he started to paddle with his left paw and off he went.

After about five minutes, Scamp realised that he was going around in circles, so he swapped paws and paddled with his right paw, hoping that would get him back on track, but he was back where he started!

Two with the right paw and two with the left, that should do it, he thought, and he was right.

Off he went, floating underneath the water, slowly crossing to the other side. Scamp was exhausted but he had done it! He had found a way to cross the Singing River. Dragging his submarine out of the water, he shook his fur until it was dry, then packed away his umbrella and string.

Carrying his suitcase under his arm, he shuffled up the riverbank and into the woods. It had been a long day and Scamp was very tired.

But which way shall I go now? he thought as he yawned, and scratched his head. As he did so, something soft and fluffy tickled at his nose.

Feathers carry dreams, thought Scamp as he began to follow the feather that danced and swirled ahead of him in the gentle evening breeze. In the distance, Scamp could see the faintest wisp of smoke spiralling into the sky. As he got closer, he could see it was coming from a little cottage nestled amongst the trees.

Chapter 5 –

Scruffy and Scamp

The cottage belonged to a rather naughty little bear called Scruffy. It was a cosy little cottage with a star-shaped chimney which was puffing away, blowing smoke stars into the sky. Inside the cottage, Scruffy was just finishing his dinner before turning in for the night. Having finally finished his rather large dinner and dessert, he patted his tummy which was very full indeed and sighed.

Umm, that was delicious, but I think I might have room for just one more course, now what's for after dessert? he thought.

As he was rummaging in his cupboards for something extra especially sweet, he heard a knock on the door.

Who could that be at this late hour? thought Scruffy as he made his way to the door. Opening it, he saw the scruffiest little bear he had ever seen; his fur was sticking out in all directions; his jacket was falling off one shoulder and his bow was half undone around his neck.

"Hello," said Scamp. "I'm terribly sorry to disturb you, but I was wondering if I could perhaps stay here for the night. I'm trying to find my rightful name you see. I've been travelling all day and I really would be grateful for somewhere to sleep."

The poor little bear really did look very tired.

"Why of course, my dear fellow," replied Scruffy, glad of the company. "Do come in. Perhaps you would like to join me in some after dessert before you go to sleep?"

"I'd love to," replied Scamp, following Scruffy into the kitchen. "But what's after dessert?"

"Well," replied Scruffy, rummaging in his cupboards as he spoke. "It's a sort of second dessert you have after your first dessert because one dessert just never seems to be enough, it's my own invention you know."

After a couple of minutes, Scruffy pulled out some pancakes and a pot of jam.

"Perfect, I've been saving these for a rainy day."

"Oh dear, if you've been saving them for a rainy day, we'd better not have them," said Scamp, feeling a little disappointed because he was very hungry and his ninth favourite thing in the world after Christmas trees, snow, presents, chestnuts, string, marmalade, strawberries and ice cream was pancakes and jam.

"You see, it's not raining today," continued Scamp. "In fact, there's not a cloud in the sky."

"I see," replied Scruffy, peeping through the curtains as he spoke. "I'd better sort something out then. Do you have an umbrella by any chance?"

"Well, yes, as a matter of fact I do," replied Scamp, rummaging in his suitcase.

"Jolly good. Could I ask you, please, to stand outside the door, just for a moment?"

Scamp was puzzled but he did as he was asked.

"Put the umbrella up," shouted Scruffy from the kitchen window.

"But it's not rain—"

But before Scamp could finish his sentence it started raining, lightly at first then much harder until Scamp could hardly hold the umbrella above his head, it was raining so hard. Scruffy appeared at the doorway once again.

"Please, do come in from the rain or you'll get wet," he said. "Hurry up!"

Scamp shuffled into the cottage for the second time, shaking the rain from his fur.

"Was it raining out there?" asked Scruffy.

"Yes, yes it was. It was most peculiar," replied Scamp. "There's not a cloud in the sky, most peculiar indeed."

"In that case, would you like some pancakes and

jam?" asked Scruffy. "I've been saving them for a rainy day and after all, it *is* raining."

Following Scruffy into the kitchen, he saw the hose attached to the tap in the sink, and understood why it had started raining so suddenly. Smiling in silent friendship, the scruffy little bear and his naughty new friend sat down and ate a generous portion of pancakes and jam.

"I'm glad it was raining today," said Scamp as he wiped the last bit of jam from his mouth.

"Me too," replied Scruffy.

Having finished their after dessert, the two bears were very tired and both began to yawn.

"You can sleep here in front of the fire," said Scruffy. "You'll be nice and warm. If it's sunny tomorrow, we can have strawberries and ice cream for breakfast! I've been saving some for a sunny day."

With that thought in mind, Scruffy disappeared up the ladder to his bedroom and promptly fell asleep.

Scamp was tired, but as he lay in the little cottage by the fire, his eyes were wide open and his mind was full of adventure. He had achieved a lot today. He had left Willow Grove and all that he knew. He had crossed the Singing River in a floating submarine, and he'd had pancakes and jam on a pretend rainy evening with his new friend. Smiling in contentment he drifted off to sleep, dreaming of sunny days, and strawberries and ice cream.

High in the sky, the sun began to yawn. It had been a long day and the sun was sleepy.

If there's going to be sunshine tomorrow, I'd better get some sleep. It's time to wake the moon.

The sun patted her flames until they were just a dim glow and called to the moon to get up.

"It can't be time for me to get up already?" grumped the moon as he rubbed his eyes and frowned at the sun.

"Afraid so," replied the sun as she snuggled onto her cloud and curled

up her glowing flames. "I'll see you in the morning."

The moon was very lazy but he knew that if the sun had gone to sleep, then he had no choice but to get up, or there would be no light in the night sky. Slowly, bit by bit, he peeped out from behind his cloud until he was shining full and round in the cold night air.

Oh, my goodness, it's cold tonight, he thought as he shivered in the sky. *It's far too cold to be out here alone, and besides, I can't light the whole night sky all by myself.*

The moon knew that the stars loved to dance, so he called to the wind to whistle a tune. As the wind whistled, music filled the air and one by one, the stars appeared and began to dance. The more they danced, the brighter they shone, and as they jumped around with joy, swinging each other round and twinkling with delight, they lit the night sky.

Scamp woke bright and early the next morning. He was dreaming about strawberries and ice cream, and it was so real that he could almost taste them. Rushing to the window, he closed his eyes, crossed his paws and wished it would be sunny. With one eye open, he peeped through the curtains to find the sun shining, and the sky blue.

How marvellous, that means we can have strawberries and ice cream for breakfast!

He quickly pulled on his jacket, straightened his bow tie and combed his fur. Glancing in the mirror, he couldn't help but think that he looked much more like a 'Scruffy' than a 'Scamp' and that it was odd that he had met someone that was much more like a 'Scamp' than a 'Scruffy'. Very strange indeed, he thought. But his desire for strawberries and ice cream was stronger than his curiosity, so he decided to go and wake Scruffy before the sun went in.

Scruffy was already up, and was busy in the kitchen preparing breakfast.

"Good morning, my friend. Did you sleep well?" he asked as he sprinkled some sugar over a rather large bowl of ripe, plump strawberries.

"Yes, I did," replied Scamp as he eyed the juicy red berries and licked his lips. "Very well indeed. I had a wonderful dream about strawberries and ice cream, sunshine and blue sky, and then when I woke up, the sun was shining and my dream had come true!"

"Me too," said Scruffy, smiling to himself as he took a

large scoop of ice cream from the fridge.

It was then that Scamp noticed the whistling sound coming from outside the back door.

"What's that noise?" he asked as he walked towards the door.

"What noise? I can't hear anything," replied Scruffy, looking decidedly guilty.

Scamp opened the back door and looked into the garden. Standing on the grass was the strangest looking machine that he had ever seen! There was a long pipe sucking air from the sky, and lots of cogs and wheels turning round and round. On top of the machine was a funny yellow cone-shaped hat which was spinning very fast and making a *very* loud noise.

"Oh, *that* noise," said Scruffy, looking very sheepish. "That would be my sunshine-maker."

"Your sunshine-maker?" repeated Scamp. "You mean, you can actually make sunshine?"

"Of course! It's very easy really. My machine simply sucks the light from behind the clouds, spins it round in the yellow cone until it looks like sunshine, then puts it back in the sky in front of the clouds."

Scamp couldn't help but laugh, his new friend really was the naughtiest bear he had ever met. Returning to the kitchen, Scamp and Scruffy tucked into their breakfast with the sound of the sunshine-maker whistling away in the background.

The big bowl of strawberries and ice cream was finally empty, and the bears were well and truly full.

"That was delicious," said Scamp as he licked the last bit of ice cream from his lips. "But shouldn't you turn the machine off now, you don't want to annoy the sun, you know how sensitive she can be."

"Yes, I suppose I should," replied Scruffy, tentatively making his way towards the door. "She doesn't like it when I make pretend sunshine.

Last time I made some, she wouldn't come out for a week. Hopefully, she won't be up just yet."

Opening the back door, he tiptoed quietly into the garden, and hid behind his machine. Hoping that the sun wouldn't see him, he reached out and switched the machine to 'off', then quickly hid back behind the machine again and waited to see what happened. To Scruffy's despair, the whirring noise stopped but the sky stayed bright and sunny. This could only mean one thing; the sun was already up and she wouldn't be happy.

Uh oh, he thought, as he peeped out from his hiding place and tiptoed ever so quietly back towards the cottage, hoping the sun wouldn't notice. He was halfway across the garden when the sky went grey, the sunshine disappeared, and suddenly it was cold and dark outside.

Scruffy froze. *I think I'm in BIG trouble...* he was right. The sun was in a very bad mood, she had got up especially early to bring sunshine into the world, only to find that one naughty little bear had beaten her to it.

"Caught you," said the sun, frowning from behind her cloud. "Not that it matters but I was planning on being out all day today, I won't bother now, I think I'll stay behind my cloud and wash my flames instead."

"I'm really sorry," said Scruffy. "I didn't mean to upset you. I just wanted to have some sunshine so I could eat my strawberries and ice cream. Won't you come out? It's awfully cold out here."

"Won't, shan't, not coming out!" replied the sun, crossing her flames and sulking behind the clouds.

She really was most annoyed, and decided to take the rest of the day off in protest, to teach the little bear a lesson.

Scruffy sighed. The gloomy sky reflected his mood as he hunched his shoulders and walked back towards the cottage. It was cold and miserable with no sunshine in the world, and if that wasn't bad enough, all the flowers in the garden were staring at him with scowls on their faces.

"We need the sunshine to make us yellow," said the daffodils. "What are we going to do now?"

"And we need the sunshine to make us grow," said the roses. "We'll never get to be pretty if we stay so small."

Scruffy hung his head in shame. He hadn't meant to upset the sun, and he didn't want the daffodils to stay green or the roses to stay small, so he promised himself that he wouldn't use his sunshine-maker again for at least a month. Hopefully, the sun and the flowers would forgive him by then.

Returning to the cottage, Scruffy looked very sad indeed.

"Is everything ok?" asked Scamp. "It's gone awfully dark outside. Was the sun very annoyed?"

"Yes, she was. I'm in big trouble with a capital D," replied Scruffy.

"D?" questioned Scamp as he silently counted through the letters T-R-O-U-B-L-E on his paws. "But there isn't a 'D' in trouble."

"Not normally," replied Scruffy, "but 'D' stands for '*DOUBLE* trouble'. That means I'm in trouble with more than one person. The sun is angry because she got up early to make the day sunny, and now she won't come out, and the flowers are angry because they need sunshine to make them grow. If I'd known that the sun was coming out, I wouldn't have used my sunshine-maker, we could still have had our strawberries and ice cream and I wouldn't be in double trouble!"

"Oh dear," said Scamp, trying not to smile because poor old Scruffy did look very sad. "Don't worry, I'm sure the sun will forgive you soon, she loves to shine in the sky so she won't stay away for long. Maybe next time you want strawberries and ice cream you should wait for the sun to come out first? My friend the Professor told me that the longer you wait for something, the better it tastes, and if you want something badly enough, then you just need to dream about it and eventually it will come true."

"Really?" said Scamp, feeling better already. "I've got some chocolate mousse that I've been saving for a windy day. Do you think if I dream about the wind tonight then the wind will come tomorrow, and I can eat my chocolate mousse?"

"Oh yes," said Scamp, "and if it doesn't come tomorrow, just dream about it again and again, and eventually the wind will come. Just think about how much fun you can have making your dreams come true."

"How exciting!" said Scruffy, faking a yawn as he started to plan his dream about windy days and chocolate mousse. "Actually, I do feel a little weary today, I think I'll get an early night tonight so that I can dream extra especially hard."

Scamp smiled. It was time for him to go. He still had a long journey ahead of him, so he needed to get a move on before he wasted the day. He quickly packed his suitcase, adjusted his bow tie and combed his fur.

Turning to Scruffy, he thanked him for his kindness.

"I won't forget you," he said, as he walked towards the door.

Scruffy didn't want him to go, he liked his new friend and if truth be told, he was a bit lonely all on his own in his little cottage. But, at least now, he had his dreams to look forward to, so he didn't feel quite so bad.

"Where exactly are you going?" asked Scruffy, following his friend to the door.

"I'm not sure," replied Scamp. "But I'm sure I'll know when I get there.

Waving goodbye, he promised to come back and visit soon, then shuffled off down the hill as fast as his little paws would carry him.

Chapter 6 –
The Crossroads of No Return

It was a cold and gloomy day; the sky was grey and the world was draped in a blanket of sadness. The sun was still in a bad mood, and sat behind the clouds, twiddling her flames but she couldn't resist a quick peep through the clouds every now and then to see what was going on in the world.

Scamp walked for miles and miles, he walked so far that his poor little legs ached. Over fields and hills, on and on he walked, he didn't stop for a minute.

"My word," exclaimed Scamp. "That's the second furthest I've ever walked in my entire life. I must be nearly somewhere by now."

He was, for unbeknown to Scamp, he had walked all the way to the Crossroads of No Return. Right in front of him were four different roads, each with a different signpost and each with a differently named path to take.

Oh no, he thought. *What do I do now? If I take the wrong road, then I'll never find the Name Maker and I won't get to find my rightful name.*

Fiddling nervously with his bow tie, he looked at the four different roads and read each of the signposts out loud. The easy road was signposted to nowhere, the soft road to elsewhere, the hard road to somewhere and the difficult road to anywhere. It was all very confusing.

Scamp knew that only one of the four roads would lead him to where he needed to go, so he had to be sure that he chose the correct one. *But how can I choose when I don't even know where I'm going?* thought Scamp as he scratched his head!

Looking up to the sky, he called for the wind to help.

"What shall I do, wind?" he asked, in the hope that the wind would help him.

SOMEWHERE

NOWHERE

ELSEWHERE

ANYWHERE

"What are you thinking?" replied the wind.

"Thinking?" repeated Scamp. "Oh dear, I thought you might ask me that. Well, you see, I just can't help it, I'm thinking about Christmas again, with snow and presents under the tree, and I know I shouldn't but… I'm thinking about chestnuts."

"CHRISTMAS AND SNOW?" bellowed the wind. "That's not going to help you now, think again!"

Oh my, thought Scamp, as he shook his head from side to side to try and stop himself thinking Christmas thoughts.

Standing under the cold, grey sky, he suddenly felt very alone and wished he was safe and secure back at the old bakery in his coal bucket, warm and cosy beside the fire. But he had come so far, he couldn't give up now, so he closed his eyes and tried to think really hard about what he should do.

Strawberries, no that won't do. Honey and bicycles, no that won't help. Oh yes, I know! Popcorn! No, that's not it.

He walked backwards and forwards, sideways and back again, trying to think what to do but still nothing came to him.

"I know, I'll stand on my head and see if that helps," said Scamp.

"Good idea," said the wind.

So, stand on his head he did. Suddenly, the world looked different, sort of upside down and back to front, everything seemed to be the reverse of what it was. Standing on his head under the cold, grey sky, Scamp thought what to do.

If everything is in reverse, then the easy road will be hard and take me to nowhere, and the hard road will be easy and take me to somewhere.

He didn't know exactly where he was going, but he did know that he was on his way to somewhere, he also knew that getting this far had been hard, and this was also a hard choice to make.

'Following your dreams won't be easy,' the dream had said, it all made perfect sense.

That's it! I'll take the hard road to somewhere. Why of course!

Jumping onto his paws, happy once more, he turned left onto the hard road and carried on his way. Scamp shuffled down the road as fast as his little legs would carry him. He walked past forests and rivers, hills and fields; on and on he walked until his poor little legs ached but he didn't stop for a minute.

Chapter 7 –
Lucky Cows

"My word!" exclaimed Scamp. "I must be nearly somewhere by now."

He was, he had nearly walked all the way to the field of lucky cows. Gradually, the hard road to somewhere got narrower and narrower until it became a small path weaving in and out of the forest. Scamp was puzzled but carried happily on his way until the path got so narrow that he could barely walk along it. At the end of the path was a large rock with the words 'Do you feel lucky?' engraved on the surface.

Underneath the rock, there were two arrows, one that said 'yes' which pointed to the left, and one that said 'no' which pointed to the right. Scamp frowned as he stared at the words on the rock.

What a strange question, he thought. *Do I feel lucky? Well, let's see. It was lucky that I managed to stay awake to find the Dream Machine, and it was lucky that I managed to cross the Singing River in my floating submarine, and I suppose it was lucky that I met my friend Scruffy, and had*

pancakes and jam on a pretend rainy evening, and strawberries and ice cream on a sunny morning, and I suppose it was lucky that I chose the hard road to somewhere. So yes, I think I do feel lucky, he concluded, with a nod of his head.

Happy with his decision, he turned left onto the 'yes' path and carried on his way. After a couple of minutes, the path began to widen again, getting wider and wider until it opened up to reveal a large, rose-covered arch and a lush, green field beyond.

I wonder what's through there, thought Scamp as he stopped to admire the plump, fragrant roses which twisted with velvety softness around the arch. *What pretty roses! They must have had plenty of sunshine,* he thought as his little nose sniffed at the delicate scent in the air.

The roses made him think of his friend Scruffy, and his sunshine-maker, and he hoped that he was having lots of fun dreaming of windy days and chocolate mousse. Walking under the arch, Scamp crossed through to the other side and as soon as he did so, the clouds disappeared, the sky turned blue and the sun shone brightly.

The field was full of cows. But these were no ordinary cows. Unbeknown to Scamp, he had entered the field of lucky cows. Each of the cows wore a coloured jacket with a number embroidered on the back in gold thread. Some wore daisy chains around their necks, and others had brightly-coloured feathers woven into their hair.

Feathers carry dreams, thought Scamp as he walked into the field. It was a beautiful flower-covered field, full of happy, colourful cows, laughing and playing as they chewed on the grass and lazed under the trees, sheltering from the sun.

In the far corner beyond the field, Scamp could see a kind of merry-go-round, and hanging above the wheel, suspended on a long chain, was a large golden hoof which glistened in the sunlight as it dangled in the air.

As he made his way towards the centre of the field, one by one, the cows stopped what they were doing and turned to see who had come to visit them on this lucky day.

"Hellooooo," said one of the cows, swinging her tail as she sauntered towards him. "I'm Buttercup."

"And I'm Clover," said another, following close behind. "Who are yooooou and what brings you to the field of lucky cows?"

Scamp fiddled nervously with his bow tie, took a deep breath and replied. "Pleased to meet you both. My name's Scamp. I'm terribly sorry to disturb you, but I'm on my way to find the Name Maker. I've crossed the Singing River in a floating submarine, and I took the hard road to somewhere and then, when I was nearly somewhere, I took the 'yes' path at the 'do you feel lucky?' rock and it led me here.

"I wonder if you could tell me the best way to get to the Alphabet Forest? You see, I need to find the Name Maker, there's something very important that I need to ask him, something very important indeed."

Clover and Buttercup looked at each other and frowned.

"And why would a little bear like you need to see the Name Maker?" questioned Clover, as she lowered her face, and looked him squarely in the eye.

Scamp swallowed, the cows were much bigger than him and he couldn't help but feel a little bit frightened. Taking a deep breath and standing as tall as he possibly could, he replied.

"Well, it's like this you see. I don't feel like a Scamp, I don't think that I look like a Scamp, whereas all my friends, well, they all look like who they are... Oh, except my friend Scruffy, that is, he doesn't really look like a Scruffy at all... Anyway, I need to find the Name Maker because... well, because..."

Standing on tiptoe, so no one else could hear, Scamp whispered in Clover's ear, "I think that I may have been given the wrong name."

"Oh dear!" replied Clover as she raised her head and gave Buttercup a knowing look. "You poor, wee thing. What a terrible business, a terrible business indeed."

"Oh yes," agreed Buttercup, shaking her head from side to side, "a terrible business."

"So you see," continued Scamp. "That's why I need to find the Name Maker: he's the only one who can help me. If you could just tell me the best way to the Alphabet Forest, I'll be on my way."

The two lucky cows looked at each other and nodded.

"Will you excuse us a moment? We just need to have a wee chat. Come on," said Buttercup, beckoning Clover with her tail.

The two lucky cows turned around and took a few steps forward to discuss the situation in private.

"He doesn't really look like a Scamp, does he?" said Clover, looking over her shoulder and eyeing the little bear up and down as she spoke.

"No, not at all," replied Buttercup, shaking her head. "He's a scruffy little thing if you ask me."

"My thoughts exactly," said Clover. "We'd better take him to the Lucky Wheel."

"You're right, there's nothing else for it," agreed Buttercup.

The two cows walked back towards Scamp.

"Come with us," said Clover. "We're going to take you to see Madame Moolina. She's the head of the lucky cows, she'll be able to help you."

"Come along now, mooooooove along," they said, as they trotted off in the direction of the merry-go-round.

"Wait for me," shouted Scamp, as he shuffled along behind. The cows were very large and they walked much faster than he could, so his little legs had to move twice as fast to keep up.

"Who is Madame Moolina and how can she help me?" asked Scamp, struggling to keep up with the two cows.

"She's the queen of the lucky cows, the head of the herd," replied Buttercup.

"The keeper of Hector's hoof, lady luck herself," added Clover. "She's French royalty, you know... and she's the guardian of the Lucky Wheel which leads to the Square Lake... which leads to the Magic Gate... which leads to the Alphabet Forest, where the Name Maker lives."

How strange, a French-speaking cow, he had never met a French speaking cow before... I wonder if she's ever seen a Christmas tree and snow, and I wonder if she likes marmalade, thought Scamp as he shuffled along, lost in his Christmas thoughts.

Before long, they reached the edge of the field, and a gap in the hedge that led to Madame Moolina's private garden and the merry-go-round spinning wheel thing.

"In you come," said Clover.

"Breathe in," said Buttercup as the two cows squeezed through the gap in the hedge.

Scamp smiled, he was much smaller than the two cows and could fit through the gap quite easily. Stepping through the hole in the hedge with plenty of room to spare, Scamp entered the most beautiful garden he had ever seen. It was lush and green, and the grass was soft and spongy beneath his paws, like a thick velvet carpet. Framing the lawn in a circle of rainbow colours, clusters of flowers swayed gracefully in the gentle breeze.

In the far corner of the garden sat Madame Moolina, who was busy polishing her Lucky Wheel. She was a beautiful cow with big brown eyes framed by long spiky lashes. Her hair was immaculately combed, her hooves were painted pink, and there was a matching bow securing her neatly-plaited tail.

"Bonjour, my little friend," she drawled in her thick French accent as she rose from her resting place and sashayed regally towards Scamp,

her tail swinging with every step that she took. "Let me introduce myself: I am Madame Moolina, keeper of the Lucky Wheel, late wife of Hector the Great – God rest his hoof – head of the lucky cows, queen of all things lucky."

Lowering her head so she could look the little bear in the eye she continued. "Tell me, what is it that I can do for you this fine and lucky day?"

"Very nice to meet you, Madame," replied Scamp, bowing as he spoke. He had never met a French cow before and wasn't entirely sure how he should behave. "I'm on my way to the Alphabet Forest to see the Name Maker. Buttercup and Clover thought you might be able to help me, if it's not too much trouble of course?"

"Non, non, no trouble at all," replied Madame Moolina, flicking her tail. "It is my pleasure to help if I can but it is not up to me. It is up to Hector and his lucky hoof."

Hanging her head, she continued with a tear in her eye.

"My dear, departed Hector, he was a fine figure of a bull. So handsome, so clever and so very lucky, he could always pick a winner and now his hoof lives on. Come, come, let us see if luck is with you today. I will call the cows to the wheel, and let Hector's hoof decide your fate."

With that, she turned, walked towards the golden hoof, stood directly underneath and let out the loudest 'MOOOOOOO' that Scamp had ever heard.

One by one, the lucky cows appeared as they squeezed through the gap in the hedge, and lolloped their way across the garden towards the wheel. Lining up in an orderly fashion, they saluted the Golden Hoof, stood to attention, then turned their heads towards Madame Moolina and waited for instructions.

"Lucky cows, at ease. Take your places; the little bear needs our help; it is time to see if luck would have it, please be seated."

Each seat had a number painted on the back, and one by one, the cows jumped on the seat that corresponded with the number embroidered on their jackets. Once in place, Madame Moolina walked around the merry-go-round inspecting her troops.

"Very good, very good," she drawled as she circled Hector's wheel to ensure that each cow was in the correct position and that all was as it should be.

Once satisfied, she stepped onto the wheel, walked to the centre and proceeded to pull on Hector's hoof. As she did so, the wheel began to spin, slowly at first, then faster and faster, until it was spinning so fast that everything blurred into a swirling circle of vibrant colour. With the wheel in full motion, Madame Moolina turned to Scamp and with a flick of her head, motioned for him to step forward.

"Come, come, my friend, it is time," she drawled as she jumped off the wheel and spun on her hooves. "Oh, la, la! Now it is up to Hector to decide. You must choose a lucky number and wait and see if Hector's hoof picks the same. He can always pick a winner, so you must think very carefully before you choose. If you are correct, then you may enter the Magic Gateway and luck will be with you for the rest of your journey. And if you are not, then you will have to return to where you have come from and your journey will come to an end."

Scamp swallowed. *Oh my*, he thought as he tried to think what to do. *My dreams have brought me so far, but if I pick the wrong number, then I will have to return to Willow Grove and I'll never get to see the Name Maker and find my rightful name. But how do I choose? I have come so far. I cannot turn back now.*

Scamp stared at the wheel, narrowed his eyes and tried to follow it as it spun round and round but it was making him dizzy and all he could see was a swirling mass of colour. Looking up to the wind in the hope that he would be able to help him, he asked:

"What shall I do wind?"

"What are you thinking?" came the reply.

"Thinking?" repeated Scamp. "Oh dear, I thought you might ask me that. I can't help it, I'm thinking about Christmas again, with snow and presents under the tree, and I know I shouldn't but… I'm thinking about chestnuts."

"CHRISTMAS AND SNOW AGAIN?" bellowed the wind. "That's not going to help you now, think again!"

Oh my, thought Scamp as he shook his head to try and empty it once and for all of Christmas thoughts. *Chocolate, no that won't do. Toast and marmalade, no that won't help. Oh yes, I know, ice cream. No, that's not it.*

He walked backwards and forwards, sideways and back again, trying to think what to do but still nothing came.

"I know, I'll stand on my head and see if that helps."

"Good idea," said the wind.

So, stand on his head he did. Suddenly, the world looked different, sort of upside down and back to front, everything seemed to be the reverse of what it was. Lost in his upside-down thoughts, Scamp forgot about Madame Moolina and Hector's wheel and closed his eyes to concentrate on the task at hand.

If everything is upside down, then my favourite number which is nine because it's the closest you can get to ten without being ten, becomes a six. When I entered the field of lucky cows, I counted six cows and Buttercup was the sixth cow I counted, and she wears a number six. I also have six things in my bag and marmalade is my sixth favourite thing in the whole wide world. There are nine letters in marmalade and Clover wears number nine, and nine upside down would be a number six... It all makes perfect sense! That's it! Number six, why of course!

Jumping onto his paws, happy once more, Scamp turned towards Madame Moolina and tugged on her tail.

"I know! I know!" he said, jumping up and down. He was so happy; he could barely contain his excitement. "It's six. Number six."

"Is that your final answer?" questioned Madame Moolina as she sauntered back towards Hector's wheel.

"It is," shouted Scamp as he followed close behind.

"Very well then, let's see if Hector agrees."

With that, she let out the second loudest 'MOOOOOOOOOOOOOOO' that Scamp had ever heard. As she did so, the wheel gradually began to slow down, slower and slower, until Scamp could finally see the individual cows and make out the numbers on their backs. As the wheel ground to a complete standstill, Hector's hoof also came to a stop and pointed directly to Buttercup and the number six.

As the wheel stopped, the lucky cows all turned their heads to look at the little bear who stood wide eyed, with his gaze fixed directly on Hector's hoof.

"Did I win?" asked Scamp, still a little dizzy from watching the wheel spin.

"Yes, my friend. You did," replied Madame Moolina, with a flick of her tail. "It is done, you are officially lucky, and Hector has once again picked a winner – God rest his hoof. You are now free to continue on your journey. Follow the 'I am lucky' path and it will take you where you need to go."

Scamp jumped up and down with joy. He had done it; he had found the lucky number and would soon be on his way to see the Name Maker and find his rightful name. All the cows gathered round and danced about, swinging their tails as they wished him well on his journey.

Chapter 8 –

The Square Lake

"Oooo la la, it's going to be a full mooooooooon tonight. I do love to listen to moooosic in the mooooonlight," drawled Madame Moolina as she danced around the wheel, spinning on her hooves.

"My dear Hector, how he loved to dance, he was a real mooooover you know?"

Scamp smiled; it was time for him to go. Picking up his suitcase, he stood on tiptoe and gave Buttercup and Clover a big hug.

"Feathers carry dreams, you know?" said Buttercup as she plucked a feather from her hair and handed it to Scamp.

"Thank you so much for your help, I couldn't have done it without you."

The two cows blushed, and fluttered their big eyes as Scamp kissed them both on the cheek.

"I'll never forget you. Farewell, my friends," he said, as he shuffled down the 'I am lucky path', following the feather as fast as his little paws would carry him. Scamp walked for miles and miles, he walked so far that his poor little legs ached. Over fields and hills, on and on he went, he didn't stop for a minute.

"My word," exclaimed Scamp. "That's the third furthest I've ever walked in my entire life. I must be nearly somewhere by now!"

He was, for unbeknown to Scamp, he had walked all the way to the Square Lake.

Standing at the edge of the Square Lake, Scamp scratched his head.

He was puzzled. He had never seen a square lake, all the lakes he had seen before had been round. But it was a beautiful square lake, surrounded by lush velvety grass and brightly coloured flowers in all different shapes and sizes.

In the centre of the lake, suspended in mid-air, was a shiny, gold gate which sparkled and glistened in the afternoon sun.

That's very pretty, I wonder where it goes, thought Scamp as he walked closer towards the gate. As he did so, far in the distance, he could see a signpost saying 'Alphabet Forest only twenty-six letters away'.

Why that's it! That's where I need to go, to the Alphabet Forest to find the Name Maker.

So off he went, walking round the lake towards the sign. He walked for a bit, then turned left, then turned right, until he was on the opposite side of the lake. Looking up, he expected to have reached the signpost, but it had disappeared. Looking back to the opposite side of the lake, the sign was there.

How strange, thought Scamp as he carried on walking, right then left, until he was back where he started.

But again, when he looked up, the sign for the Alphabet Forest was on the other side of the lake where he had just been. Scratching his head, Scamp was very confused.

I'm sure that's where I've just been, he thought and turned to go back once again but the same thing happened.

Suddenly, the air filled with the sound of laughter. Looking around, Scamp saw that all the flowers around the lake were holding their leaves over their faces and giggling uncontrollably. Scamp frowned, he didn't like being laughed at and he didn't see what was so funny. All he was trying to do was to reach the signpost on the other side, so he could get into the Alphabet Forest and find the Name Maker. Turning to the nearest sunflower he asked,

"What's so funny? Why are you laughing at me?"

"I'm sorry," replied the flower. "It's just that you

could be here all day if you keep going the way you're going."

"But how do I get to the Alphabet Forest?" asked Scamp. "Every time I try to reach the signpost, it moves. I don't understand. It's very annoying."

"Don't you know?" replied the sunflower. "You need to go round the lake and through the Magic Gate, only then can you enter the Alphabet Forest."

"But if the lake is square then how can I go round it?" asked Scamp, frowning as he spoke. "And how am I going to go through the Magic Gate when it's

up there?" he asked as he pointed to the gate hanging in the air.

"That's for me to know and you to find out," laughed the sunflower, tickling her stem as she giggled with delight.

Scamp was tired and hungry and didn't know what to do. Sitting down at the lake's edge, he suddenly felt very alone. He was a long way from home and he missed the Professor and all his friends back in Willow Grove. He missed his coal bucket by the fire, and his woolly sock which was the most comfortable place in the whole world.

I wonder what time it is, thought Scamp as he hung his head.

As he sat hunched and lonely by the edge of the lake, he heard the Professor's words echoing in his head, 'If it's cold, then it's time to get warm and if you are hungry, then it's time to eat.'

That's it, thought Scamp, *I need some marmalade, I always feel better when I'm eating marmalade.*

Opening his suitcase, he took out his jar and scooped out a generous portion, then another and another until he was well and truly full.

That's much better. Now, where was I? Oh yes, I remember. I need to get to the Alphabet Forest but the sign keeps moving. Oh, and I need to go round the Square Lake and through the Magic Gate but it's square and the gate is in the air, so how am I going to do that? It's all most confusing!

As he was thinking what to do, a small, fluffy, white feather danced in the air and tickled at his nose before it floated towards the sky, higher and higher as the wind carried it towards the Magic Gate. 'Feathers carry dreams', the Professor had said, so he stood up to follow the feather as it danced in the wind and began circling the gate.

As the wind got stronger, the feather swirled faster and faster around the gate, beckoning him to follow. Scamp called to the wind in the hope that he could help.

"What shall I do, wind?" he asked.

"What are you thinking?" whispered the wind in reply.

"Oh dear, I knew you were going to ask me that. It's not that I mean to, and I do keep trying really hard not to, but I'm thinking about Christmas and snow and lots of presents under the tree wrapped in shiny gold paper… and I know I shouldn't but I'm thinking about chestnuts roasting on the fire."

"CHRISTMAS AND PRESENTS? That won't help you now, think again," said the wind. Scamp scratched his head and tried to think really hard.

Ok, strawberries and chocolate? No, that won't help. Ice cream and popcorn? No that's not it. How about a rainbow? No that's not it either, thought Scamp as he paced up and down.

He walked backwards and forwards, sideways and back again, but still nothing came.

"I know! I'll stand on my head and see if that helps."

"Good idea," said the wind.

So, stand on his head he did. Suddenly the world looked upside down and back to front, everything seemed to be the opposite of what it was.

If the lake is square, then I can't go round it on the outside, so I need to find a way to go round it on the inside, and if the gate is in the air, then I need to find a way to go round it in the air and the only way to do that is to fly. If I'm flying, I can make plane circles, everybody knows that!

Then suddenly the answer came.

I know, I'll make myself a balloon plane. That way I can fly round the lake and through the Magic Gate. Why of course, that's it. Why didn't I think of that before? Looking up to the sky, he thanked the wind, then off he went to build his balloon plane.

First of all, I'll need a licence, I can't fly a plane without a licence, he thought, so he rummaged in his suitcase to see what he could find.

Pulling out his picture, he smiled. *This will be perfect but I need to make it official.*

Scamp dipped his paw in the lake, rubbed it in the mud and stamped it on the back of his picture. Satisfied that he could now officially fly, he removed his jacket, buttoned it up and stitched the hem and cuffs together with some string, leaving a small gap in the seam so that he could inflate it with some air.

That can be my balloon, he thought. *Now what shall I fly in?*

Emptying his suitcase, he opened it as wide as he could, then sat in it.

Perfect, that can be the cabin. Now all I need are some propellers and then I'm done, so off he went to find some wood.

Rummaging in the bushes, he found two long, thin twigs. Returning to his plane, he tied the twigs loosely to the front of his suitcase with his remaining string, and spun them round to make sure they worked properly.

Fantastic! He had built himself a balloon plane. All he needed now was some hot air then he could take off and fly round the lake, through the Magic Gate and into the Alphabet Forest beyond.

But where can I get some hot air from? he thought, scratching his head.

The sun wasn't shining, so she wouldn't be able to help. He didn't have a cooker nearby, so he couldn't boil some air to make it hot.

Oh dear, thought Scamp. *What am I to do? I know! I'll run around really, really fast, get very, very hot, then blow all my hot air into the balloon jacket, that should do it.*

The wind whispered in silent agreement, so off he went running around in circles as fast as his little paws would carry him. On and on he ran, round and round, backwards and forwards, jumping and skipping, up and down and down and up. He ran until he was so out of breath and so hot that his fur was sticky with sweat and he could run no more.

Huffing and puffing, he stopped and felt his forehead.

Oh yes, he was very hot, very hot indeed. *It doesn't get much hotter than this,* he thought.

Satisfied that he was as hot as he could possibly get, he held his breath, shuffled over to his balloon jacket, and blew all his hot air into the small gap he had left in the seam. As he did so, his jacket got bigger and bigger and gradually started to float in the air.

Holding on to the balloon-jacket sleeve, he stepped into his cabin and slowly his balloon plane began to rise. Up and up it went until it was floating high above the lake. Leaning out of the cabin, Scamp flicked the propellers until they were spinning round, and as they began to spin, the plane began to move, slowly at first, then faster as the propellers gained momentum. Leaning to the left, the plane began to circle the lake, leaning to the right and then to the left until Scamp was flying round in balloon circles.

As he completed his first circle, the Magic Gate began to open, a little bit at first but with each plane circle he made, the wider the gate opened and the faster he circled, the quicker it opened until it was open wide.

As he flew through the gate, the lake faded away and instead Scamp could see a forest of lush green trees each with clusters of small and capital letters hanging off the branches. As he glided deeper into the forest, his hot air began to cool and as it did so, the balloon plane

gently floated down towards the ground, until with a thud, he landed next to a bush of 'S's, which smelt so sweet and succulent that Scamp licked his lips as he sniffed the air, absorbing the sugary scent. He had done it. He had gone round the Square Lake in balloon circles and flown through the Magic Gate into the Alphabet Forest where the Name Maker lived.

Chapter 9 –

The Alphabet Forest

Nestled amongst the Letter Trees, in the old Alphabet Forest, was the Furry House on the hill. It was a funny little house with a furry roof and spiral chimney. At the front of the house, the big red front door was peppered with 26 multi-coloured letter boxes and a sign above saying 'post your letters in here'. Inside, the Name Maker sat quietly by the fire, sipping his cup of T's, staring at the flames as they danced and swirled, teasing the wood as it burned.

Tomorrow was a very important day: it was Sunday. The Name Maker knew it was Sunday tomorrow because he had had an E, two G's and an S for breakfast, and he always had that for breakfast on Saturday. Sunday was naming day, so he had to make sure that he ate plenty of letters for dinner so that he had lots of names ready-made in his tummy to name all the new-born bears.

The Name Maker was a funny old man, with a big nose and thick, curly, grey hair. His face was softly wrinkled and his big eyes seemed to smile from beneath his bushy eyebrows as they twinkled with mischief. He always wore a very tall pinstripe hat to cover a bald patch at the top of his head, and on naming days, he wore his special black and white printed alphabet jacket which was always neatly washed and ironed for the occasion.

He had a busy day's naming ahead of him, so he needed to make sure that he ate a balanced diet of vowels and consonants. If he didn't, he wouldn't be able to make enough names, and if he ate too many of any one letter, then he would get all his names mixed up, and that wouldn't do at all.

It was getting late. He just had enough time to pick some fresh letters from the Alphabet Forest before the sun went to sleep and the moon woke up, so he pulled on his fur-lined coat to keep him nice and warm for his letter picking.

Oooooh, I feel just like a bear, he thought, as he wriggled into the fur and snuggled into its softness.

Opening the door, he walked up the furry path, through the gate and into the mumbling hills beyond where the alphabet trees grew. The closer he got, the louder the mumbling became, as all the letters shouted out in the hope that they would be chosen.

"Choose me", "no choose me" … "me" … "no me", they all said, trying to persuade him to choose them for his name-making.

It was a great honour to be chosen for name-making, so they all tried very hard to get picked. As the Name Maker walked past a bush of R's, he could smell raspberries and rosemary, then a bush of C's which smelt of chocolate and coffee; it was all so tempting and was making him feel very hungry.

Although all the letters smelt good, nothing compared to the smell of the letter S. As he got closer, he could smell strawberries and Smarties, sugar and syrup; it was so strong that he began licking his lips; he could almost taste the sweetness. Reaching up, he quickly grabbed a handful of S's then turned away before he was tempted to take any more. Going back to the A's he took a couple, then a U and on he went until his basket was well and truly full. Satisfied that he had a good selection of letters, he turned back onto the furry path, and made his way back to his cottage to bake his letter pie for dinner.

Returning to the furry cottage, he placed the basket on the table.

*Now, what shall I have tonight? h*e thought as he sorted through his freshly-picked letters. *Two A's, a U, a G, one E and an S, or maybe two? Oh, go on then, just one more,* he thought as he plucked a third S from his basket.

Arranging his letters in the pot, he checked to see what he had for dinner. S-A-U-S-A-G-E-S. *Oh yes, that sounds very tasty, very tasty indeed.*

The letter S was his favourite, it was so sweet and sugary and just so easy to swallow, and it smelt soooo good. The more he ate, the more he wanted and the more he wanted, the more he ate, and this was the problem. So, before he was tempted to add a fourth S to the pot, he put it into the oven and went into his chamber to polish his naming pipe. The pipe had to be clean and shiny, so that when he spoke into the pipe, the names would slide down easily and could be clearly heard during the naming ceremony. If there was even just a small amount of dust inside, it could affect things quite badly, and if he ate the wrong mix of letters, then it could affect things very badly indeed. By the time he had finished cleaning his pipe, his dinner was ready, so off he went to eat.

"Ummm," he said as he took another mouthful, "if only I had a few more S's, then this would be just perfect." The sad truth was that he knew he could not: if he didn't eat just the right balance of vowels and consonants, then he would get all his names mixed up and cause terrible confusion like he had five years ago. He was still haunted by the memory, those poor little bears with the wrong names, and all beginning with the letter 'S'. He felt very bad that he had given them the wrong names, but they would never know, and he would never tell, so he just had to learn from his mistakes and never do it again. So, without giving it another thought, he proceeded to finish his meal.

It was getting late and the Name Maker was tired; his naming pipe was clean and he had a tummy full of letters, so it must be time for bed. Climbing the stairs to his sleeping chamber, he changed into his nightshirt and got into bed. His tummy was very full. As he closed his eyes, and drifted off to sleep, he could hear his stomach rumbling and mumbling as all the letters that he had eaten slowly turned into names, ready for the naming ceremony in the morning.

Scamp was also tired, he had come a long way on his journey, he had chosen the right path at the Crossroads of No Return, entered the Field of Lucky Cows, picked a winner at Hector's Hoof, built a balloon plane, flown round the Square Lake and through the Magic Gate and into the Alphabet Forest.

It had been a long day and the sun's flames were beginning to fade in the evening sky. The shadows of the day played hide and seek, darting in and out of the light as they teased the sun, and tried to stay awake. Scamp yawned, he knew it was time for bed so he dismantled his balloon plane, packed everything back into his suitcase and looked around for a place to sleep.

In the distance, a large bush of Z's swayed tantalisingly in the evening breeze. The sharp edges of the letters glistened in the fading light and jingled together like tiny bells. The melodic sound of the Z's jangling in the wind was like a soft lullaby calling to him, so off he went shuffling down the Mumbling Hill towards the Z bush and into the Alphabet Forest beyond. The closer he got to the Z bush, the softer the ground became until Scamp was practically bouncing with every step he took – boing, boing, boing – down the hill.

The ground around the bush of Z's was very soft and springy, like a musical mattress.

This is the perfect place to sleep, thought Scamp as he put down his case, bounced up and down on the springy ground and made ready for the night.

"Good idea," whispered the wind in silent approval.

Nestling under the bush, with the sound of the Z's lulling him to sleep, Scamp curled up, snuzzled into the springy softness, closed his eyes and promptly fell asleep.

The evening sky was nearly dark. The sun was busy putting out her last few flames, but before she was quite finished, the moon was already awake and bouncing impatiently in the sky behind her. The moon was looking forward to going out tonight because there was one little star who had danced so prettily and sparkled so brightly to light the night that it had caught his eye. Smoothing his hair, he quickly checked his reflection in the Singing River before he rolled off his cloud and jumped into the night. The sun was most confused and checked her position in the sky, the moon was early, there must be something wrong.

"My dear friend," said the sun. "You don't need to come out for at least another ten minutes. Are you feeling alright? And, if you don't mind me saying, you look very handsome tonight."

"I do? Well, one does need to make an effort sometimes," said the moon coyly, blushing as he spoke.

As the moon blushed, the sky turned a deep shade of red, and a warm glow filled the night sky.

"I must have got my times mixed up," continued the moon. "Still, I'm up now so why don't you put your flames out and have an early night, I can take over from here."

"That's very kind of you," replied the sun as she patted the last of her flames until they were well and truly out. "I'll see you in the morning then."

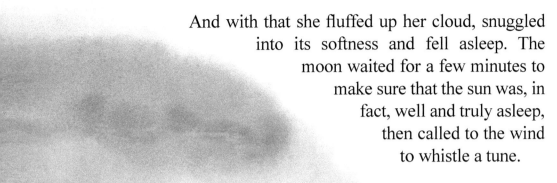

And with that she fluffed up her cloud, snuggled into its softness and fell asleep. The moon waited for a few minutes to make sure that the sun was, in fact, well and truly asleep, then called to the wind to whistle a tune.

As the wind whistled, the music filled the air, one by one the stars appeared, and began to dance. The moon looked around, eager to find his special star, and seeing her twinkling in the sky as she laughed and danced around, his heart filled with joy and the moon smiled big and round for the world to see.

High in the sky, the sun was sleeping peacefully on her cloud as the moon and the stars danced through the night to the tune of the whistling wind. It was nearly morning; the moon was tired and the stars were beginning to fade, as they had been dancing all night. The moon kissed his little star 'goodbye' and as he did so, the sky blushed a faint shade of pink which mingled with the first morning light as the sun stretched her flames and bounced into the sky ready to light the day.

Chapter 10 –

The Name Maker

Scamp was already awake. There was something tickling his nose, and there was an awful lot of noise. Opening his eyes, he saw the feather dancing in the wind, teasing him to get up.

Feathers carry dreams! thought Scamp, as he blinked in the morning sunlight and rubbed his eyes. All around him, the sound of the alphabet letters swaying in the wind beckoned him to get up and follow the feather's lead.

Wiping the sleep from his eyes, Scamp suddenly remembered where he was and excitedly hopped onto his paws and scratched at his nose.

Oh my, he thought, the time has finally come! I've made it to the Alphabet Forest and it's time to meet the Name Maker and find my rightful name. Packing away his things, Scamp brushed his fur, straightened his bow tie and set off down the hill, following the feather's lead as fast as his little legs would carry him. He walked past trees of A's and B's, W's and D's. On and on he walked, his poor little legs ached he had walked so far, but he didn't stop for a minute.

"My word," exclaimed Scamp. "I must be nearly somewhere by now."

He was, he had walked all the way through the forest and to the Name Maker's house beyond. In the distance, Scamp saw the strangest house he had ever seen. It had a furry roof and a furry door and a long, tall, spotted chimney puffing smoke words into the air. 'H E L L O... W E L C O M E'

the smoke letters said. Shuffling down the hill until he was standing at the door, Scamp froze. He was a long way from Willow Grove and his coal bucket by the fire. What if the Name Maker wasn't in, or worse, what if he didn't remember him…or even worse, what if he didn't live here at all!

"Don't be afraid," whispered the wind as he gently nudged him closer towards the door with a little puff. The sun peeped through the clouds and smiled in silent approval.

Taking a deep breath, Scamp filled himself with courage and knocked on the door.

After a few seconds the door slowly creaked open.

"Well, hello Scruffy, how nice to see you after all these years," said the Name Maker, smiling warmly as he looked at the little bear with his jacket half undone and his fur sticking out in all directions.

"Very nice to meet you, Mr Name Maker sir, but I'm afraid you've made a mistake, my name isn't Scruffy," corrected Scamp politely as he fiddled with his bow tie. "It's *Scamp*."

"What! It's not Scruffy?" The Name Maker frowned. "But I'm never wrong about these things, it's my job you see. Are you sure? Are you completely sure?" he continued as he bent down to look the little bear squarely in the eyes.

"Well, yes... and no, it's complicated," replied Scamp, as he fidgeted uncomfortably under the Name Maker's stare.

Ummm, that's strange, thought the Name Maker as he stroked his pointy chin. *Very strange indeed.*

Putting on his best authoritative voice, the Name Maker continued rather gruffly, "You don't look like a Scamp to me but if you say so, please do come in and tell me what it is I can do for you on this fine day."

Stepping into the furry house, Scamp was suddenly very shy. What if the Name Maker couldn't help him, and what if Scamp really was his rightful name? What if he had emptied his thoughts in the Dream Machine, crossed the Singing River, picked a winner at Hector's Hoof and made balloon circles round the Square Lake all for nothing!

"Please, do sit down and warm yourself by the fire," said the Name Maker, as he put a pot of water onto the stove.

"Can I interest you in a cup of T's?"

"Oh no, thank you," replied Scamp. "I won't take up too much of your time, I just wanted to come and see you because I need to find the answer to my question, I really do hope that you will be able to help me, I've come an awfully long way."

Taking a deep breath, Scamp continued. "It's like this you see, I don't feel like a Scamp, I don't look like a Scamp and well... all my friends, they look like who *they* are." Standing on tiptoe so no one else could hear, Scamp whispered in the Name Maker's ear,

"I hope you don't mind me saying, but I think that I may have been given the wrong name."

"Wrong name?" repeated the Name Maker. "This is a very serious accusation. I will have you know that I don't make any mistakes when it comes to naming, I am very careful about these matters and it would be most irregular to have given you the wrong name, most irregular indeed. I always make sure that I eat a balanced diet of vowels and consonants the night before naming, I hand pick each letter myself from the Alphabet Forest and won't let anyone else touch them for fear of contamination."

"I make sure that my naming pipe is clean and polished, so that it is silky smooth to ensure all the names slide down easily without any problems, and I *always* go to bed really early to allow sufficient time for the rumbling and mumbling, so that the letters get well and truly mixed up in my tummy. So, you see, it just isn't possible that there has been a mistake. I am sorry to say that you have had a wasted journey, but it has been lovely to see you after all these years, you have grown into a very polite young bear. I am proud of you," the Name Maker concluded as he slapped Scamp affectionately on the back.

Scamp's shoulders slumped as the full impact of the Name Maker's words sunk in. All these years, he had been convinced that he had been given the wrong name. Scamp just didn't feel right, it didn't fit, it didn't match his reflection and he simply didn't feel like a Scamp at all but if the Name Maker said it was right then it must be true.

Wiping a little tear from his eye, he walked slowly towards the door. It felt like the weight of the world rested on his little shoulders as he turned the handle and walked outside, to begin the long journey back to Willow Grove.

He suddenly felt very alone, and wished that he was safe and secure, tucked up inside his sock in his coal bucket by the fire.

"Thank you, Mr Name Maker sir," he said as he waved goodbye. "I won't take up any more of your time. I'm sorry that I doubted you, I see now that I shouldn't have. I did have a lot of fun following my dreams, and at least I have found the answer to my question, although it is not the answer that I wanted, but it is better than no answer at all."

"Quite right," answered the Name Maker as he patted the little bear on the back. "Now now, no need to be sad, young fellow. Off you go," he said as he followed Scamp out of the door to see him on his way.

The Name Maker felt strangely sad as he watched the little bear shuffle down the path. It did seem very odd to him that the little bear was called Scamp. He looked much more like a Scruffy to him, and he couldn't imagine for the life of him why he would have named him Scamp. Turning towards his naming pipe, he scratched his head and paused for a moment of thought and suddenly a thought came; it was a big thought, a very, VERY big thought, bigger than the biggest thought he had ever had.

Rushing outside, he ran up the path behind him. "Oh no! Wait a minute," he shouted. "How old did you say you were?" called the Name Maker as he turned to size up the little bear.

"I think I'm five," replied Scamp, counting the number of birthday cakes he had ever eaten on his paws. "Yes, five." At that moment, the Name Maker went very pale as the memory of his over indulgence five years ago came flooding back.

"Oh dear, oh dear," he said as he paced up and down. "This won't do, this won't do at all. I cannot lie to you. I believe you might be right after all. I think I have made a terrible mistake."

Turning to look him in the eye, the Name Maker took a deep breath, and continued.

"You should have been called Scruffy, it's obvious to me and probably to everyone else, and it's my fault, but the S's, they are so temptingly sweet and sugary, and they smell of strawberries and syrup. They are so very hard to resist and I am a weak man. I couldn't help myself you must understand, they are just too tempting. One terrible day, five years ago, I ate too many. I didn't think it would matter, but in all the rumbling and mumbling in my tummy, the names must have got mixed up.

"I only named a few little bears that day, I knew something was wrong, so I stopped my naming ceremony as soon as I realised. I had hoped you and the other bears would never find out, that you would grow into your names and be none the wiser. Can you ever forgive me? I am on a strict diet of vowels and consonants now, so it will never happen again, I can assure you of that!"

Grinning from ear to ear, Scamp was filled with joy. He knew in his heart that he wasn't *really* a Scamp and the Name Maker had now confirmed it. He couldn't contain his happiness now that he had found his rightful name. "Scruffy? WHY YES, THAT'S IT! I AM SCRUFFY! That feels just right. No matter what I do, I always look scruffy, my bow tie is always half undone, my fur sticks out in all directions and my pyjamas always seem to go on back to front. I look like a Scruffy, I feel like a Scruffy, so I MUST BE a Scruffy. It all makes perfect sense!" Everything felt just as it should be.

After the initial excitement subsided, Scamp began to frown... he was a bit confused.

"But, Mr Name Maker sir, if I am called Scruffy, then my friend Scruffy can't be called Scruffy, so that means he must be called Scamp. Why of course! He looks just like a Scamp and he behaves like a Scamp, so I'm sure he won't mind if we swap names. It is my rightful name after all, I'm sure he won't mind if I have it back."

"What a splendid idea," agreed the Name Maker, relieved that he could finally right the wrong caused all those years ago. Using his best, serious, listen-to-me-carefully, stern voice, he continued.

"You must get his permission first of course, and not use your rightful name until you have officially swapped with it Scruffy. Naming is a very important business and regulations have to be followed. We need to do these things properly; I do hope you understand. So... unless he agrees to give your name back to you, I'm afraid you can't have it."

"I will, Mr Name Maker sir," replied Scamp, "I promise."

"Good, that's settled then, we'll hear no more about it. Before you go, will you join me for lunch? I have a capital-letter casserole that's ready to eat. You'll need to get your strength up for the journey, there are lots of healthy vowels in there to keep you going."

"Thank you, yes please," replied Scamp. He was very hungry after all the excitement of the day and the capital-letter casserole did smell very good.

Sitting by the fire in the Name Maker's kitchen with his tummy full of healthy vowels, Scamp smiled in silent contentment. He had followed his dreams to find his rightful name, he had found a way to overcome his fears and find the answer to his question and he was truly at peace with himself. No longer would he worry about his fur being straight, his bow tie being half undone or his pyjamas being inside out and back to front. He was called Scruffy after all! *That's how I'm supposed to look,* he thought.

The sun smiled proudly in the sky, her flames radiating a soft amber glow as the wind blew a gentle breeze in silent agreement.

Chapter 11 –

Windy Days and Chocolate Mousse

It was time to go. Picking up his suitcase, Scamp gave the Name Maker a farewell hug and thanked him for all his help. Opening the door, he stepped onto the furry path then shuffled up the hill into the Alphabet Forest and the mumbling hills beyond. A single feather danced in the wind. *Feathers carry dreams,* thought Scamp, as he followed its lead. He walked for miles and miles and his poor little legs ached. Before he knew it, he was back at the Square Lake, and walking down the windy lane and into the field of lucky cows.

"Hello, Madame Moolina!" shouted Scamp.

"Bonjour my little friend," replied Madame Moolina as she sashayed across the field with her neatly-plaited tail swinging rhythmically behind her, with Clover and Buttercup following close behind.

"Hello," said Buttercup.

"Hello little scruffy bear," said Clover. "We wondered when you would come back with your rightful name."

"But how did you know Scruffy was my rightful name?" replied Scamp a little puzzled.

"Well, it was obvious to us that you were never a Scamp," said Buttercup.

"Och no," agreed Clover.

"NON!" agreed Madame Moolina with flick of her tail. "Anyone with any sense could see that you were a Scruffy, mais oui, it was obvious to us and the hoof of Hector is never wrong, oh non, never."

"Thank you all for your help, especially you, Madame Moolina," said Scamp curtsying as he spoke. "I couldn't have found my name without you, or your dear departed Hector of course – God rest his hoof. But I'm afraid I can't stay for long. I'm on my way to see my friend Scruffy so that we can swap names. I need to follow regulations to make it official, otherwise I can't have my name back. It's a serious business and I promised the Name Maker, so I'd better get a move on before the sun goes to sleep. I'll never forget you," he continued, as he hugged Buttercup and Clover goodbye and carried on his way.

Before he knew it, he was back at the Crossroads of No Return but the signposts had changed. This time they read; 'The easy road from somewhere, the soft road from elsewhere, the hard road from nowhere and the difficult road from anywhere.' Scamp turned right at the Easy Road from Somewhere because he knew he had come from somewhere, and he knew that this time the journey would be easy because he had found his rightful name and was going home to Willow Grove. On and on he walked, his poor little legs ached but he didn't stop for a minute. Gradually, the sun began to fade. In the distance, Scamp could see big grey clouds twisting and swirling around the sun, dark and foreboding like angry frowns floating in the sky. It was very, very windy. The leaves of the

trees were rustled and tousled by the powerful gusts and the branches bent in submission. The light was fading but he could just about see Scruffy's little cottage in the distance.

Battling against the wind, Scamp finally managed to make it down the hill. Standing outside the door to Scruffy's cottage he was very dishevelled with his fur sticking up in all directions and his bow tie completely undone. *I do feel very scruffy today,* he thought with a smile, *but I don't care! I'm proud to be Scruffy, I like*

being Scruffy and soon I will be able to tell all my friends, just as soon as I have swapped names and made it official. He had come a long way since he last saw his friend. What if Scruffy didn't want to be called Scamp and refused to let him have his name back? His journey would all have been for nothing; it didn't bear thinking about.

"Be brave," whispered the wind as the feather danced in the wind and tickled at his nose.

But I'm not brave, thought Scamp... or am I? well... I did find the Dream Machine and emptied all my questions inside, that was brave. I crossed the Singing River and picked a winner at Hector's hoof, that was brave. I chose the right road at the Crossroads of No Return and flew round the Square Lake in my balloon plane...and that was brave. Then I met the Name Maker in the Alphabet Forest and found my rightful name. I was very scared but I did it anyway, so YES, I think I am brave after all!

Without further hesitation he took a deep breath to fill himself full of courage and knocked on the door.

"Well, hello Scamp," said Scruffy, smiling as he opened the door. "What are you doing back here so soon? I was just about to tuck into some chocolate mousse. Will you join me? I've been saving it for a windy day and as you can see, it is very windy."

"Yes, it is," agreed Scamp, looking around suspiciously for some kind of wind machine as he stepped inside the cottage.

"You don't need to worry about that," said Scruffy. "This is proper wind. Since you left, I've spent all my time dreaming about windy days just as you told me, and then this morning, I woke up and it was as windy as can be. So, you see, it does work, if you want something badly enough and dream about it really hard, then your dreams can come true."

"It's so good to see you again, my friend. Please do sit down," continued Scruffy as he motioned to Scamp to take a seat by the fire. "I'll get the chocolate mousse."

Within a moment, he was back, carrying a very big bowl overflowing with the lightest, airiest, chocolatiest moussiness that Scamp had ever seen.

"I must say, old chap, you are looking very scruffy today, is everything alright?" asked Scruffy as he paused to take in his friend's particularly scruffy appearance.

"Oh yes, everything is just as it should be," replied Scamp as he dipped his paw into the chocolatey moussiness and gave it a lick. "But there is something that I need to tell you."

"Go on," said Scruffy, as he, too, took another large scoop of mousse.

Taking a deep breath, Scamp closed his eyes and crossed his paws. "Well, there is no easy way for me to tell you this, but… do you remember being named?"

"Not really," replied Scruffy. "But I do recall it was a very short ceremony. Only a few bears were named that day, if I remember correctly, it was most unusual. I remember that the Name Maker stumbled and bumbled and seemed quite out of sorts."

"That's right," continued Scamp, pacing up and down as he spoke. "The truth is, five years ago, the Name Maker did a very bad thing, a very bad thing indeed. He ate too many S's and they had a terrible effect on him, he got a very bad case of the jollycollywobbliness and had to stop his naming ceremony. You see, the S's, they are so sweet and sugary and soooo tasty, they are very hard to resist." Pausing as he glanced back at Scruffy to make sure he was paying attention, Scamp continued. "It was a moment of weakness, but it had terrible consequences. He has assured me that it will never happen again, he is now on a strict diet of vowels and consonants, and has well and truly learnt his lesson."

"I'm very glad to hear it," mumbled Scruffy, with his mouth full of chocolate mousse. "But what has that got to do with me?"

"Well, here's the problem," continued Scamp. "Because there were too many S's in all the mumbling and rumbling in his tummy, all the names got mixed up and well... in all the confusion it seems possible... I mean it's highly probable... in fact very likely... that we were given the wrong names. My name should have been Scruffy and your name should have been Scamp."

For a moment the world stood still. The sun tentatively peeped out from behind her cloud, the wind held his breath, and the moon opened one eye, as they watched and waited to see what Scruffy would do.

"You mean I should be called Scamp? Are you sure?" he questioned, as he scratched his head and thought for a moment. "Umm, I'm not sure I like that. Oh no, I don't think I do, I think Scruffy is a much nicer name and besides, it's too late now, what's done is done. We'll just have to make the best of it," he concluded as he dipped his paw into the chocolate mousse for the third time, not giving it another thought.

Once again Scamp's shoulders drooped and his heart sank. He hadn't thought for one minute that Scruffy wouldn't want to swap names, he assumed that there wouldn't be a problem.

Scamp was totally befuddled. What should he do now? Calling to the wind in the hope that he could help him, he asked, "What shall I do, wind?" but there was no reply. The wind was too busy outside howling and growling, and didn't hear his plea. "Err hello, what shall I do, wind?" repeated Scamp as he peeped outside to see what was going on. But still there was no reply. Scratching his head, he was most confused. This had never happened before; what was he to do? *Well, there's nothing else for it, I'm going to have to think for myself,* he concluded with a nod of his head. So, think for himself he did. *What am I thinking?* he asked himself. *Well, I'm thinking about Christmas and snow, oh, and presents and chestnuts!* he replied. *No, no, that won't do,* he told himself shaking his head to rid himself of Christmas thoughts. Think again! Scamp scratched his head and tried to think really hard. *Ok, strawberries and chocolate? No that won't help. Ice cream and popcorn? No, that's not it. How about a rainbow? No, that's not it either,* thought Scamp as he paced up and down. He walked backwards and forwards, sideways and back again, but still nothing came. *I know! I'll stand on my head and see if that helps.* So, stand on his head he did. Suddenly the world looked upside down and back to front, everything seemed to be the opposite of what it was. *So, if Scruffy doesn't want to change names, it's because he thinks I want to be called Scruffy, but if he thinks that I don't want to be called Scruffy, and am happy being called Scamp, then it might make him want to be called Scamp instead of Scruffy. Why that's it! I'll make him think that I don't really want to swap names and then he's bound to want to swap, he always wants what he can't have!* Happy that he had found the answer, he jumped back onto his feet and shuffled over to Scruffy who was now licking the last remnants of mousse from the bowl. Taking a deep breath, Scamp paused for a moment as he fiddled with his bow tie.

"Of course, old chap, I mean it is the name you were given after all, so I can understand that you want to keep it. Besides, now I come to think of it, I'd much rather be called Scamp. As Scamp, I can have so much more fun. I can have pancakes and jam on a pretend rainy day, I can make sunshine when I want and have strawberries and ice cream any day I choose, oh, and I can have chocolate mousse on a windy day, so I think it would be much better to be called Scamp after all. I'm going to start enjoying myself so much more now that I know I can have all that fun."

Picking up his suitcase he turned towards the door. "It's been lovely to see you again but it's time for me to go now, so I will bid you farewell and be on my way."

Pancakes... strawberries and ice cream... chocolate mousse? But that's what I do! thought Scruffy, as he suddenly realised that everything Scamp had said fit him perfectly! "Wait a minute," he called out as he followed his friend to the door. "Let's not be too hasty. You took me by surprise that's all," continued Scruffy with a mischievous twinkle in his eye as he thought about all the naughty things he could do if he officially became Scamp. He had always been a bit naughty but somehow, having it made official seemed so much more appealing.

"I had never thought about it before, but now you come to mention it I do feel like a Scamp, I act like a Scamp and all my friends, they think I am a Scamp; therefore, I must be! So, I think I would like to swap names after all, it only seems fair, please say we can? Pleeeeeeease!"

"Well, only if you are sure?" replied Scamp, trying not to smile. "Yes, I am, I really am," replied Scruffy. He was already planning his next invention, so he could have toasted marshmallows on a snowy day, and could hardly contain his excitement.

The two friends smiled at each other as they turned to look themselves up and down in the mirror. The time had come. Touching their paws together they sealed the deal.

"Well, that's it then, it's official! I've found my rightful name, and yours has been returned to you, and all is as it should be," said Scruffy for the first time with his rightful name. The wind breathed a sigh of relief and the sun smiled brightly in silent agreement.

"So what time is it now?" asked Scamp, as he continued to admire his reflection in the mirror, thinking how well his proper name suited him.

"I think it's time to go home to Willow Grove," replied Scruffy. "I need to tell the Professor and all my friends. You must come too; please say you will."

"Of course," replied Scamp. "I'd be delighted. I'll just pack my case then we can be on our way."

Chapter 12 –

Dreams Do Come True

Scruffy was nearly home. Soon he would be back in his coal bucket, tucked up in his sock nestling beside the fire. He had missed the Professor and all his friends back in Willow Grove. He had missed his woolly old sock which to him was the most comfortable place in the whole world; even more comfortable than the springy bush of 'Z's which was very comfortable indeed.

As he turned the corner into the cobbled square, all the townspeople came out to greet him. They knew it was time for him to come home.

"Hello, old friend, we've missed you, welcome home!" they shouted.

Shuffling up to the old bakery door, he stepped inside.

" W e l c o m e home, Scruffy, nice to meet you,

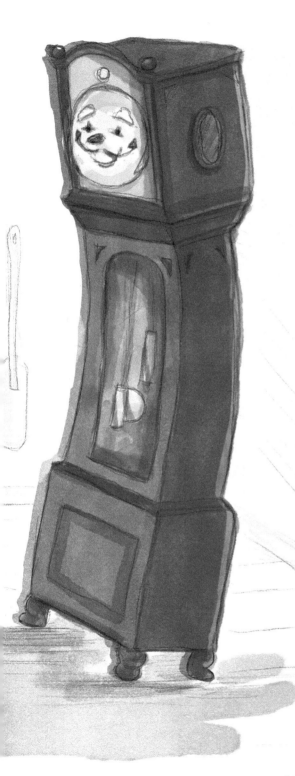

Scamp," said the Professor as he clapped his hands together and let out a welcome home chime. The Professor knew Scruffy now had his rightful name because the Professor knows everything about everything!

"Please come in from the cold. We have a Christmas tree waiting with presents wrapped in shiny gold paper for you and I was just about to roast some chestnuts on the fire."

"Christmas tree!" exclaimed Scruffy. "Presents and chestnuts! Why that's everything I've ever dreamed of!"

A soft, fluffy, white feather tickled at his nose.

Feathers really do carry dreams, thought Scruffy as he followed its lead and stepped inside.

The Professor smiled as he watched the two little bears. Scamp and Scruffy warmed themselves by the fire as they roasted chestnuts and stared excitedly at the presents wrapped in shiny gold paper sitting under the tree. The wind whistled, quietly at first, then louder as it called to the two friends to look outside. Scamp jumped onto the window ledge and cleared a patch on the steamy window with his paw.

"Come see, come see," he said, bobbing up and down excitedly as he called to Scruffy to join him.

"What's going on?" replied Scruffy, who was busy shaking his presents for the fiftieth time, trying to guess what was inside.

"Look outside," said the Professor. "And you will see."

Scruffy reluctantly put his present down and jumped onto the windowsill next to Scamp. Outside, the cobbled square was draped in a beautiful blanket of snow; crisp and white, it covered the world with its delicate softness. Across the cobbled square, the street lights flickered in the distance casting a warm glow while the snow gently fell to the ground like little white diamonds dancing in the night.

"Oh my!" exclaimed Scruffy. "It's snowing, it's really snowing! I've never seen snow before, or had a present under the tree wrapped in shiny gold paper, or roasted chestnuts on the open fire. All my dreams really have come true!"

He was right. The two little bears smiled at each other as they stood by the window, excitedly watching the snow fall. Scruffy and Scamp, each with their rightful name.

The sun slept peacefully on her cloud and the moon shone high and proud in the sky, with his little star twinkling beside him. The wind blew a gentle breeze teasing the snow as it fell to the ground, and all was still in Willow Grove.

The End

I hope you enjoyed
my adventure.

scruffy x

…Anything is possible if you follow your dreams

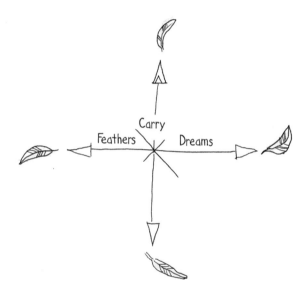

With special thanks to
Joanna Scott and Alex Young
for their unwavering patience and support.